The Mixed-Up Rooster

Written by Pamela Duncan Edwards

Illustrated by Megan Lloyd

KATHERINE TEGEN BOOKS
An Imprint of HarperCollinsPublishers

Library of Congress Cataloging-in-Publication Data
Edwards, Pamela Duncan.
   The mixed-up rooster / written by Pamela Duncan Edwards ; illustrated by
Megan Lloyd.—1st ed.
      p.   cm.
   Summary: Ned the rooster is fired from his job because he cannot wake up in
the morning, but he restores his reputation after discovering his usefulness as a
night bird.
   ISBN-10: 0-06-028999-6 (trade bdg.) — ISBN-13: 978-0-06-028999-7 (trade bdg.)
   ISBN-10: 0-06-029000-5 (lib. bdg.) — ISBN-13: 978-0-06-029000-9 (lib. bdg.)
   [1. Roosters-Fiction.   2. Chickens-Fiction.]   I. Lloyd, Megan, ill.   II. Title.
PZ7.E26365Mix 2006   2005014401
[E]—dc22   CIP
                                                                               AC

Typography by Jeanne L. Hogle
1 2 3 4 5 6 7 8 9 10

First Edition

For Mike and Libby Mahr——what fun we've had!
——P.D.E.

To Tom, who checks the chickens every night.
——Love, M.L.

A ray of sunshine found its way through a crack in the henhouse door and landed on Daisy Mae's face.

"Cluck! Cluck!" cried Daisy Mae. "Wake up, everyone!"

"Is breakfast ready?" asked Mildred.

"No time for breakfast," clucked Daisy Mae. "Ned's overslept again."

A rooster who was perched in the corner snored loudly.
Daisy Mae gave him a sharp peck.

"Take that, you lazy rooster," she cackled. "What happened to heralding the dawn? Cock-a-doodle-doo and all that stuff? You've made us late for work again."

"Oh boy!" groaned Ned. "I can't help it, Daisy Mae. I'm just not a morning bird, that's all."

"You're a completely mixed-up rooster, that's what you are," cried Daisy Mae.

"Zzzzzzzzzz," snored Ned.

"That's it," screeched Daisy Mae, pecking Ned again.
"You're fired. You're ruining my egg business."

"Oh, come on, Daisy Mae," yawned Ned. "I'm not that bad."
"Not that bad!" squawked Daisy Mae. "You're hopeless!
What's the use of a rooster who can't wake up at the right time?"

"It's not worth getting your feathers ruffled," said Ned. "OUT!" cried Daisy Mae. "Mildred, get the head office on the phone. Tell them we need a regular rooster down here immediately. Not one who sleeps in every day!"

"Okay then," cried Ned. "I've had enough of this henpecking. I'm off!"

Ned fluttered to a high branch and looked down on the farmyard. "Daisy Mae's got a good head for business," he grumbled. "But she sure is a nag."

Ned watched as another rooster strutted up to the henhouse.

"Cock-a-doodle-doo!" called the rooster.

"Oh boy," said Ned. "He's good!"

Ned spent the day sulking in the tree until the dusk became night. Soon all was quiet in the henhouse.

"Psst!" whispered a voice in the dark.

"Who's there?" gasped Ned.

"Bats," replied the voice.

"Rabbits," said another.

"Tree frogs," said a third. "Want to play?"
"Oh boy," said Ned. "Do I ever."

Then Ned became a real night bird.

He played tag with the bats.

He danced ring-around-the-rosy with the rabbits.

He sang with the tree frogs.

They all had a swooping,
hopping, wonderful time.

"Let's play hide-and-seek," announced a tree frog. "Ned can be It."
"Oh boy," said Ned, hiding his eyes. "This is going to be fun."
He couldn't see that one of the rabbits had raised its white
bobtail, signaling danger.

"Here I come, ready or not," said Ned.
There was silence except for the sound of
creep, creep, creep.
"I can hear you! You can't fool me," called Ned, laughing.
When Ned opened his eyes and looked around . . .

his feathers stood on end. A long, black snake was slithering
quietly toward the henhouse.

"Oh boy!" gasped Ned. "He's after Daisy Mae's eggs. The new
rooster forgot to close the henhouse door. It's all up to me!"

Ned crowed as he had never crowed before.

doodle-doo!
Cock-a-doodle-doo!

Snake
Attack!"

Dust flew as he frantically swooped down and
scratched the dirt in front of the snake.

"A-A-A-A-CHOO!" sneezed the snake.

Daisy Mae scrambled through the henhouse door.
She pecked the snake hard.

"Ouch!"

howled the snake,
slithering off into
the night.

Inside the henhouse, panicked hens ran this way and that.

"Calm down, everyone!" cried Daisy Mae. "The crisis is over. Ned saved us!"

"Hooray for Ned!" cheered the hens.

"Just look at that pesky new rooster," tutted Daisy Mae in disgust. "He slept through the whole thing."

"Don't be hard on him, Daisy Mae," said Ned. "He's just not a night bird, that's all."

"Will Ned get his job back now?" asked Mildred.

"No way," clucked Daisy Mae. "I've got a much better job for Ned."

"Oh boy, Daisy Mae!" crowed Ned.